CHAPTER ONE
Thick snow and burnt toast

O'Donnell opened one eye, yawned, and scratched his ear with his paw. O'Donnell was an Irish wolfhound, though oddly enough he had never been to Ireland and had never seen a wolf. He was thinking how cold it felt for a July morning. It was shiversome!

When he looked out of the window he got a terrible shock. Tibbenham Common was completely covered with snow!

3

O'Donnell gave an excited growl and
rushed to his owner's bedroom, but he
found it was empty. She had vanished!
He was just going to call a police-dog

when he heard the
sound of the front
door and the tramp
of familiar feet.
It was his owner,
Rebecca.

Forecast
of Fear

Permission to land!

St Mary Magdalen's
R.C. Primary School,
Worple Street,
London SW14 8HE

Keith Brumpton

Young Lions

JUMBO JETS
Bernie Works a Miracle by Leon Rosselson
Fergus the Forgetful by Margaret Ryan
Forecast of Fear by Keith Brumpton
Sir Quentin Quest Hunts the Yeti
by Kaye Umansky

First published in Great Britain by
A&C Black (Publishers) Ltd 1992
First published in Young Lions 1993
10 9 8 7 6 5 4 3 2

Young Lions is an imprint of the Children's Division,
part of HarperCollins Publishers Ltd,
77–85 Fulham Palace Road, London W6 8JB

ISBN 0-00-674561-X

Printed and bound in Great Britain by
HarperCollins Manufacturing Glasgow

And yet the weather systems indicate that it should be warm and sunny!

Rebecca Farren-Hyte was a weather-girl for the local TV station. She was more interested in the weather than anything else in the world. Without even looking in her notebook she could tell you the temperature on Tyneside, the wind-speed in Watford, or the rainfall in Rotherham; not to mention hurricanes in Honolulu or precipitation in Prestatyn. In other words, when it came to the weather, Becky was a grade one expert.

O'Donnell thought all this weather talk was pretty boring. What did it matter so long as it was nice enough to go for a walk or chase rabbits on the moor?

'This is very serious,' sighed Becky, not noticing that her breakfast toast had caught fire. 'All our forecasts for this week have been completely wrong. The weather seems to be going crazy! The last time we had snow in July was in 1852. There were two centimetres on the weather-vane of Exeter Cathedral.'

O'Donnell began to whine, and pointed to the toaster with his paw.

'Oh crumbs, burnt the toast again!'

Slice of Mighty Black

CHAPTER TWO
Snow on the roses

Before going to work, Becky always went down into the garden and studied her various instruments for measuring the weather. She had wind socks . . .

← No, not on her feet!

and weather-vanes, rain-water gauges, and even a few strands of seaweed (a traditional method of forecasting the weather).

Today she spent longer than usual double-checking her measurements.

A worried look came over her face.

O'Donnell was rolling in the snow (a great way to get rid of an itch).

'According to all my calculations, the weather today is actually 20° centigrade. In other words, very warm.'

Rebecca turned up her blue nose and looked at the mournful sky. It was a grey smudge, full of snow.

Some traditional ways of forecasting the weather

I. "Red sky at night, shepherd's delight"

Country folk say that if you see a red glow in the sky at night it means that it will be fine the next day.

← Either that or the shepherd's cottage is on fire!

II. "A lot of berries in winter means a good summer"

Unfortunately by the time you've counted all the berries you'll probably have missed most of the summer anyway!

III. "Cattle lying down means rain on the way"

On the other hand it could just mean that the cattle are tired after a hard day's moo·ing and chewing.

A better way of forecasting rain is to look out for people putting up umbrellas.

This is usually a good sign that there's going to be a splash!!!

CHAPTER THREE
A very unpopular person

Becky and O'Donnell usually walked to the TV studios. It wasn't far and they both enjoyed the exercise. O'Donnell liked to frighten the Pekinese who lived at the bottom of the hill, whilst Becky checked over her script for the day.

Today their walk took longer than usual, partly because the snow was so deep, but mostly because people kept stopping Becky in the street.

'Hey, aren't you the weather-girl? I thought you said it would be sunny today?' snorted a man with Bermuda shorts and blue knees.

A pensioner crossed the road and told Becky that she'd hung out her washing last night, and now her best summer frock was as stiff as a board.

You could always use it to surf on...

Two young girls were in tears because their tortoise was lost in snowdrifts at the foot of the garden.

Help!

As Becky and O'Donnell walk to work things look **BLEAK!**

To Gribbledale

LADIES' FINAL

TV aerial

To Tiger Bay ←

Tennis club

TV station where Becky works

Gladacre farm

Becky and O'Donnell walking to work.

Radio Tibbenham

Daffy Duck Primary School

The High Street

'The Queen's Knees' (pub)

Batsman vanishes in blizzard!

14

'Oh dear,' groaned Becky, 'I think I must be the most unpopular person in the world right now.'

O'Donnell gave her hand a lick.

CHAPTER FOUR

Mr Hale in a stormy mood

Becky crept into her dressing room at the TV station and got changed. She didn't feel much like meeting anyone. In the corridor she could hear her boss, Mr Hale.

Mr Hale didn't like Becky very much. He said she was too young to be a weather-girl and too cheerful. He knocked on her door and peered in.

Becky felt very depressed.

'Perhaps you were looking at the wrong photos,' growled Mr Hale, 'or maybe you had them upside-down. I've had people ringing up all morning to complain.'

D'you know that two cricketers are in the local hospital suffering from frostbite?

O'Donnell thought about giving Mr Hale another sort of bite, but Irish wolfhounds are gentle dogs, so he growled instead.

GRRR

Mr Hale looked at O'Donnell nervously, then he looked at Becky.

I'm sorry, Miss Farren-Hyte, but unless your forecasts for the rest of the week are more precise...

I'm afraid I shall have to find someone else...

Someone who can inform the public more accurately!

Becky wondered what to do. Everything told her that the weather tomorrow should be warm with a little light cloud. But what if she were wrong again?

← She'd be for the high-jump!

She decided that after filming she would head off to the weather centre and talk to her old friend, Professor Byedale. Maybe he could throw some light on the situation.

Let's hope so!

CHAPTER FIVE

A ridiculously short chapter which you could read in between mouthfuls of jam doughnut

O'Donnell took his usual place next to Pete the cameraman while Rebecca did her stuff.

She stood in front of the weather chart and pointed to all the various symbols.

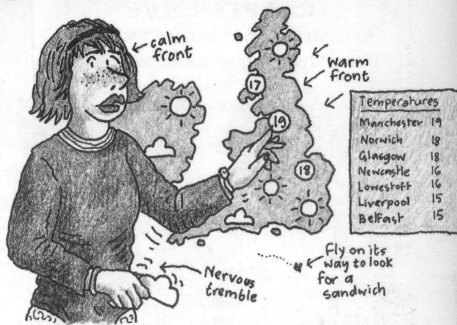

← calm front

← warm front

Temperatures

Manchester	19
Norwich	18
Glasgow	18
Newcastle	16
Lowestoft	16
Liverpool	15
Belfast	15

Fly on its way to look for a sandwich

← Nervous tremble

She wasn't her usual cheerful self. Mainly because her chart was covered with bright sunshine symbols and she had a horrible feeling that tomorrow wasn't going to be sunny at all.

Becky's nightmare

→ Wet toupee

25

And with a high pressure front settled over Britain . . .

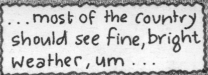

...most of the country should see fine, bright weather, um . . .

with just the odd shower, creeping in from the west.

And that's it from me until tomorrow...

enjoy the rest of your day. Now the news with Gloria...

opinions differ as to Becky's performance →

The transmission was over. The director said 'cut', and Pete the cameraman gave O'Donnell half a 'Hob-Nob' as was their usual arrangement. Becky let out a long sigh and went to get changed back into her warm winter clothing ready for the trip to see Professor Byedale at the weather centre.

CHAPTER SIX
Worry at the weather centre

Inside the weather centre, Becky and O'Donnell were in the lift which would take them to Professor Byedale's office on the sixth floor.

'Dr Byedale is one of my favourite meteorologists,' Becky confided to her canine chum. 'What he doesn't know about weather isn't worth knowing.'

I wonder if he knows much about chocolate digestives

The doors of the lift opened with a 'ding' and Professor Byedale was there to greet them. He was an old man, with white hair, a long white coat, and a pair of dirty Hush Puppies.

Jam sandwich →

My dear Becky, come in, come in...

I can guess why you've come, and yes...Your dog too. Goodness, what a size! I've seen smaller entrants in the Grand National.

O'Donnell trotted proudly into the professor's office. The office was very untidy — like a waste-paper bin on a windy night. Sheets of paper, books, diagrams, and computer print-outs were everywhere.

You look tired, Professor.

'Ah, you noticed. Of course I haven't had time to sleep. This has been an incredible week for British weather. We've broken more records than a dodgy DJ.'

Britain's dodgiest DJ, Brian Cowdrey, from North Wales. Brian owns only 3 records and doesn't like 'loud music'...

The professor picked up a piece of computer paper and waved it in the air.

MOST rainfall
HIGHEST windspeed
HEAVIEST frost
...These are not normal events, my dear !!!!

31

There were strange forces at play in O'Donnell's stomach, too. He had to have a snack soon! He began sniffing in the prof.'s pockets. When he had no success there, he switched to a cupboard by the kettle. Hey presto! There was an open packet of biscuits . . .

me again!

CHAPTER SEVEN
The prof. explains the problem

Becky and Professor Byedale were examining a huge satellite photograph of Britain.

You see, Becky, at 9 a.m. yesterday morning the skies were clear... Not a cloud in sight... But look...

photo

In this next photo, taken two hours later, we have storms everywhere!

The professor nodded.

Becky held the glass over the photograph and gave a sharp intake of breath.

'Look!' gasped the worried weather-girl.
'The storms *are* coming from one spot.'

This is what Becky and the Prof. saw.

Professor Byedale scratched his head and O'Donnell scratched his ear. 'That's our problem,' said the elderly expert, unwrapping a sweet. 'We need someone to go up there and take a look.'

I could go...

I'm not on the TV tomorrow, it's my day off.

O'Donnell and I could go and have a quick look round...

O'Donnell gave a deep sigh and rested his head on his paws. Days off were for chasing rabbits not for solving weather mysteries.

How come nobody ever asks what **I** want to do ??? !!!

tail at maximum droop

37

Professor Byedale was much more enthusiastic. 'That's great news, Miss Becky . . . I can't think of a better person to get to the bottom of this business. I shall sleep well tonight knowing that Rebecca Farren-Hyte of the Met. Office is on the case.'

Oh yes, cocoa tonight will be a pleasure.

Just then, as if to remind them of what they were up against, an icy gust of wind blew savagely against the window panes.

CHAPTER EIGHT

On the A19, heading up to Scotland

O'Donnell didn't like Becky's motor bike. It was noisy and the wind made his ears flap about like two towels on a clothes-line.

As they travelled along, the weather kept changing. It was almost as if someone were trying to get them to turn back.

Meanwhile . . .

steady 25 m.p.h

There was a dog riding that motor bike!

Nonsense, Nigel . . . I thought I told you to keep taking those tablets!

'I've never known the frontal systems to change so quickly,' gasped Becky between claps of thunder.

CHAPTER NINE
A frosty reception

Becky checked the map.

Shelter at last!

'Yes, this is it. This is Invergrundle and that must be the castle which was on the satellite picture.'

To reach it you have to pass through a dark wood filled with swaying, creaking, oak trees. The wind roars among the leaves, and the air is full of falling branches, tumbling leaves, and parachuting squirrels.

45

The weather in Invergrundle was stranger than anything they'd ever known. The rain stopped as suddenly as someone turning off a shower. Then it was so foggy you couldn't see your paws in front of your face (if you had paws that is).

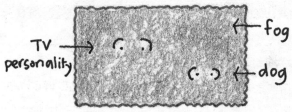

About ten minutes later, when the fog cleared, Becky and O'Donnell could see Invergrundle Castle in the distance. It was about as inviting as a ticket to watch Scunthorpe United.

Becky couldn't remember ever seeing anywhere so dark and miserable; even Count Dracula would have wanted to brighten this place up. Not only was it old and crumbling, but all sorts of strange weather seemed to hang around it: storms and thunderbolts, shafts of sunlight and sheets of black ice.

holes in roof

strange devices

windows boarded up

O'Donnell opened his packed lunch and gobbled it down. (An Irish wolfhound isn't easily put off its nosh.) After his sandwich, he felt much braver.

With a deep breath, Becky and O'Donnell crept into the windswept wood, bending into the storm as best they could, and keeping their eyes open for falling timber.

A hedgehog blew past at about twenty miles an hour, but, fortunately, he was curled tightly into a ball and landed safely on a pile of moss.

At the other side of the wood they could see a narrow, overgrown path leading to the castle.

O'Donnell calculated that if they hurried back they could still be home in time for 'Star Trek'.

Becky threw him a dark stare. 'How can you think of TV at a time like this?' she muttered. 'This weather dabbling is a matter of national importance. The safety of thousands of people may be in our hands . . .'

Sorry, or paws.

O'Donnell licked Becky's hand and they were friends again.

As quietly as two mice wearing carpet slippers, Becky and O'Donnell crept up the overgrown driveway leading to the castle.

The castle door was already open. It was a big door. You could have got a rugby team in without a squash.

But we like being squashed !!!

Tibbenham
R.F.C.

O'Donnell noticed some very strange objects.

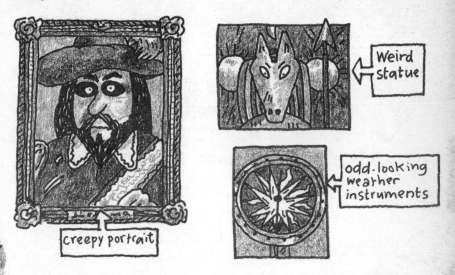

creepy portrait

Weird statue

odd-looking weather instruments

There was a high-pitched whine in the air and in the distance the sound of wind and rain, the ticking of clocks and horrible music.

TICK woosh DRIP TOCK splash HOWL whine

It was an awful combination. O'Donnell put his paws over his ears and wished he was back home on Tibbenham Common playing with Kevin the Dalmatian.

'Don't be such a puppy!' scolded Becky. 'There's absolutely nothing to be afraid of. You're a huge Irish wolfhound with big teeth, a loud bark, and if all else fails you can run off much quicker than I can.'

O'Donnell felt rather ashamed. He wagged his tail and prepared to follow his mistress wherever she might lead . . .

They crept up the stairs. But no matter how careful they were the old boards kept creaking.

Becky could only hope that the sound of the storms would drown out the sound of the stairs. When they reached the top, O'Donnell found himself beneath a small raincloud the size of an umbrella.

54

'Incredible!' gasped Becky. 'This weather really is man-made!'

And I am that man!'

replied a sinister figure, stepping out of the shadows.

Allow me to introduce myself. My name is Doctor Blizzard and you are just in time to see my invention...

only a madman would wear a bow-tie like this

before I **DISPOSE** of you both!

tight-fitting jacket

aromgter

seaweed

Becky felt worried. O'Donnell felt very worried. He'd never been disposed of before, and he didn't like the sound of it. Dr Blizzard was obviously out of his tree.

Dr Blizzard opened the door to his study and an amazing sight met their eyes. There before them stood Dr Blizzard's Incredible Bad Weather Machine.

* The Invergrundle Police have asked me to alter some parts of this drawing so that it can't be used by would-be criminals or weather-nobblers.

A powerful stream of storm clouds came out of the machine. Becky read their destination on one of the computer screens.

'Nottingham!' she gasped. 'You can't send that rain to Nottingham, it's supposed to be fine there tonight!'

Dr Blizzard laughed. A mad laugh, cold as an Arctic breeze.

You can't stop me, little Miss Farren-Hyte! You're talking to Doctor Blizzard here . . .

'Haven't you realised that I don't just observe the weather, I CONTROL it? If you want fine weather for Wimbledon or a little rain for your potatoes . . .

He's *completely* bonkers!

'Anything at all, be it frost or fog, or even hurricane, just dial Dr Blizzard and it can be arranged . . . For a very large fee, that is.'

DR BERNARD D. BLIZZARD ✳
✳ ✳ CONSULTANT CLIMATOLOGIST
Storms to order
Rainfall on request
Fog a speciality
tel 022826-43491
fax 33491-2
"Your wish is my command"

← Dr Blizzard's business card

THAT'S OUTRAGEOUS! You can't control the weather for cash. It's too important to be turned on and off like a tap. We need to have settled weather so that we can grow crops to feed people...

We plan our lives around the weather.

'I might have known you wouldn't appreciate real criminal genius,' cackled the devious doctor.

MAX TEMP 63°

He flicked a switch on his infernal machine. A great band of fog swirled out and headed towards Teeside, whilst a smaller cloud enveloped Becky and her pooch.

Becky got down on her knees where the fog wasn't so thick.

Fancy meeting you here!

On the other side of the room Becky could just make out Dr Blizzard's legs. Then, everything went white, as the fog swirled around them like smoke from a burning toaster.

Slowly, Becky inched towards Dr Blizzard's shoes . . .

IDEA

TIE LACES TOGETHER !!!

For a moment the fog cleared, and with a fearsome growl, O'Donnell leapt towards Dr Blizzard.

fierce growl

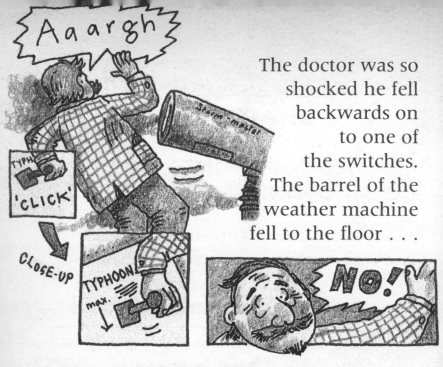

The doctor was so shocked he fell backwards on to one of the switches. The barrel of the weather machine fell to the floor . . .

Becky switched on the machine and a sudden blast of wind blew straight at Dr Blizzard, lifting the freeze-dried doc. clean through the castle roof and out over the darkening Scottish countryside.

CHAPTER TEN
Raindrops keep falling on my head

O'Donnell had just finished a couple of traditional Scottish kippers and was lying in front of the fire in Dr Blizzard's living-room. He sighed contentedly.

No time for that, O'Donnell. We still have to destroy the weather-machine, call the police, ride back to Tibbenham Common, prepare the forecast for tomorrow...

And I suppose you'll want a walk as well?

The dozing wolfhound, wagged his tail weakly.

I don't know about a walk, but I could do with an umbrella... Raindrops keep falling on my head!

THE END

If you have enjoyed the weather in this book, you might wish to see these videos produced by Tibbenham Television and featuring Rebecca Farren-Hyte.

- **GREAT FORECASTS**
- **BECKY'S TOP FORTY FORECASTS**